UNICORNS
Awesome Activity Book

Becky J. Radtke

Dover Publications, Inc.
Mineola, New York

Full of magical fun, this unicorn-themed activity book will keep you entertained for hours! More than 30 challenges include mazes, secret codes, word puzzles, hidden pictures and other baffling brain games. And the whimsical illustrations of these mythical creatures are fun to color, too. So grab a pencil and get started! If you get stuck, the answers appear in the back of the book.

Copyright

Copyright © 2018 by Dover Publications, Inc.
All rights reserved.

Bibliographical Note

Unicorns Awesome Activity Book is a new work, first published
by Dover Publications, Inc., in 2018.

International Standard Book Number

ISBN-13: 978-0-486-82807-7
ISBN-10: 0-486-82807-7

Manufactured in the United States by LSC Communications
82807706   2020
www.doverpublications.com

Connect the dots to create a beautiful creature.

Unicorns have been here! How many footprints
of each kind do you see? Write the number at the bottom.

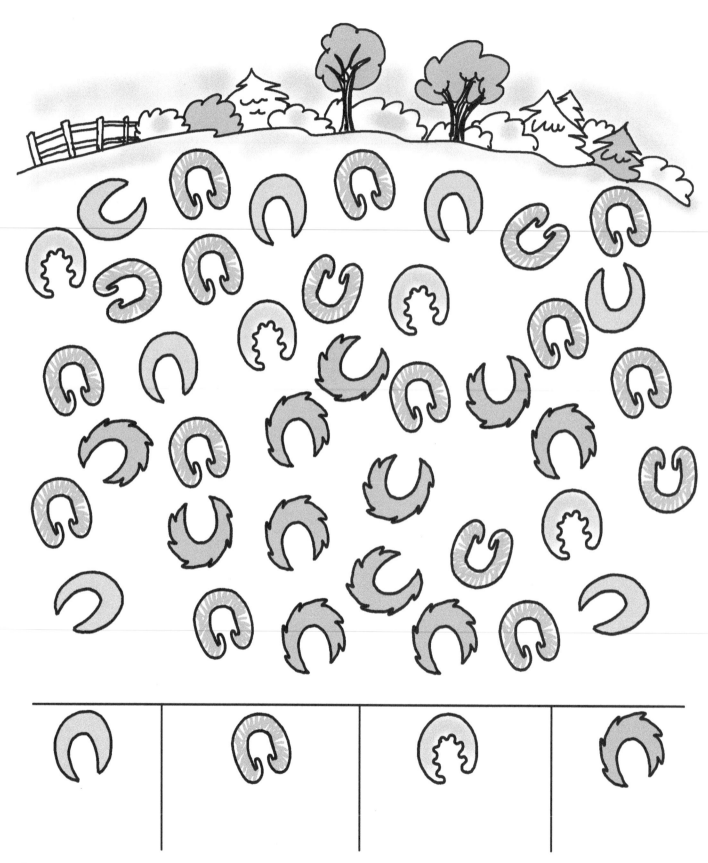

Lead this unicorn to a magical place where she can play with friends.

Fantasy Forest

See how quickly you can find and circle the crescent moon, tent, tennis ball, magnifying glass, spoon, fish, rabbit head, heart, fried egg, and hook.

Unscramble the letters to spell five words often used
to describe unicorns.

s o r h e

— — — — —

t f s a

— — — — —

e h t w i

— — — — —

n k d i

— — — — —

c a i l a m g

— — — — —

Make your own unicorn word scramble here!

The famous explorer Marco Polo once believed that he saw a unicorn! Cross out the first letter and then cross out every other letter after that. Write the remaining letters, in order, on the blanks to find out what he really saw.

— — — — — — — — — — — — —

Use the code at the bottom of the page to find the answers to these unicorn riddles.

What's the difference between a unicorn and a carrot?

  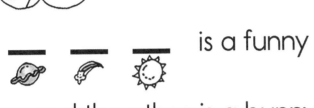   is a funny

and the other is a bunny   .

What do you call a smart unicorn?

" "

    .

Magical Code

 = E	🌍 = T	= N	= B
☆ = A	= S	= H	= R
= O	= F	= C

7

Follow the directions to lead the baby to his mother.

Shade in...
3 stars to the right
2 stars up
1 star to the left
4 stars up
3 stars right
1 star down
1 star to the right
2 stars up

Shhh! Find and circle the one sleeping unicorn that is different from the others.

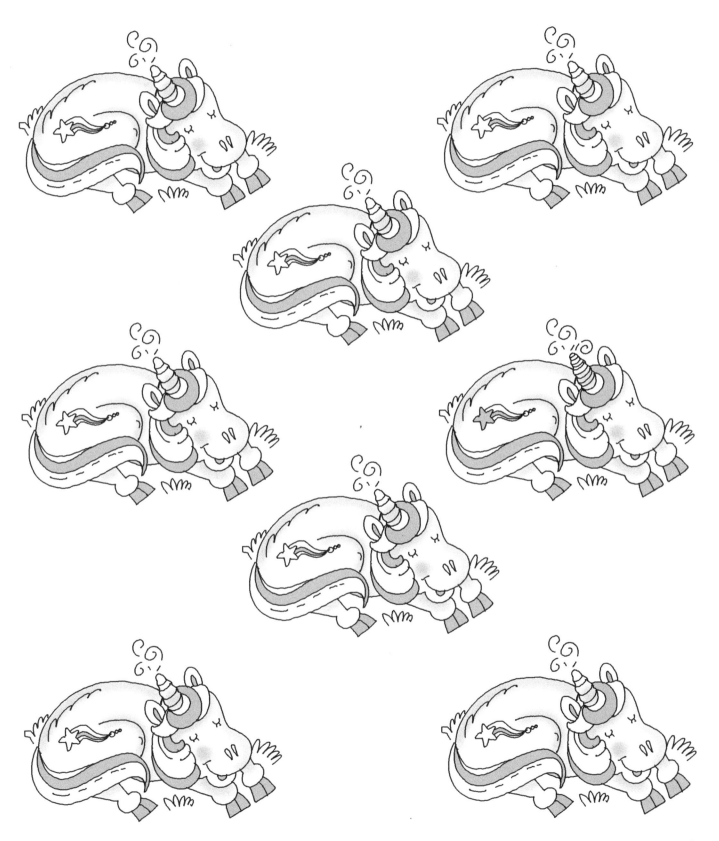

Look up, down, across, and diagonally to find and circle the word "unicorn" the number of times shown under the rainbow.

12

```
E B W G P U O Z M D E M
R N R O C I N U J H P C
U N I C O R N I L N O N
A N R O C I N U C R X L
D N R O C I N U N O P A
B Z X O Q Y M U R C R R
N Q R S Q L N Y O I C N
R N L R N T X C C N V V
O I E U C R B K I U O D
C L U O T Y O D N O R Q
I N R H I Z Z C U O J I
N N C J Q N X W I W A P
U U N I C O R N F N O D
F A U N I C O R N E U P
```

Write the letter that comes just before the one shown to reveal the name of a sea creature that is sometimes called a "Sea Unicorn."

According to mythology, what special ability do unicorns have? Use the shape code to find out.

△ = A   ◇ = M   ● = O   ♡ = S
○ = H   ▲ = I   ◆ = R   ▭ = P
☆ = E   ■ = N   ▬ = G
□ = C   ♥ = W   ★ = L

M A G I C A L

H E A L I N G

P O W E R S

12

Write the first letter of each picture clue on the space below it. The answer will tell you the kinds of colors that are said to be in a unicorn's mane. Then color the unicorn any way you wish.

—   —   —   —   —   —   —

Legend has it that unicorns can make themselves and other creatures invisible. How fast can you fit the names of these forest animals into the crossword puzzle? Some letters have been included as clues.

Write the opposite of each word on the left. When you are done, print the letters in the circles from top to bottom on the nine blank spaces below. They will spell out what it might be like to ride on the back of a unicorn.

first- _ _ _ ◯_

soft- ◯_ _ _ _

left- ◯_ _ _ _

small- _◯_ _

shiny- _ _ ◯_

dark- ◯_ _ _ _ _

out- ◯_ _

far- ◯_ _ _

stop- ◯_ _

_ _ _ _ _ _ _ _ _

Learn to draw a unicorn by following the four easy steps below. Use the empty space to practice.

1.

2.

3.

4.

Ask four friends if they believe that unicorns are real. Then fill out the graph to show the data. When you are done, write a sentence at the bottom of the page telling what *you* think.

Name	Yes	No

_____

_____

Use the vowels to finish spelling the message below. It will tell you something interesting about unicorns.

A E I O U

A GR___P
_F
_N_C_RNS
_S C__LL__D
A
BL__SS__NG.

19

Find and put a check on the unicorn that looks just like the one here. They are identical twins!

Color this picture and the one on the reverse side any way you'd like. Then cut out along the thick outer line and the dashed circle to make a hanger to put over your doorknob.

_____'s Room

Color this picture and the one on the reverse side any way you'd like. Then cut out along the thick outer line and the dashed circle to make a hanger to put over your doorknob.

Write the word "unicorn" into the boxes from top to bottom. Those letters will finish spelling seven words that are often used to describe these popular mythical creatures.

fab☐lous
lege☐dary
myst☐cal
magi☐al
h☐rse
g☐aceful
ge☐tle

You really are awesome!

I really am.

Find and circle seven things that are different in the bottom picture when compared to the top.

Circle only the capital letters in the flowered frame.
Then write them, in order, onto the blanks to find out
how long some think a unicorn lives.

unicorns are oFten shOwn as
white hoRse-like creaturEs with
a single forehead horn. almost
eVeryone has hEaRd about them.

__ __ __ __ __ __ __ __

The unicorn is just one of many popular mythical creatures. Find and circle the names of others you might have read about in well-known stories and legends. Look up, down, diagonally, forward, and backward to find the hidden words.

centaur   cyclops   dragon   fairy   gnome

gorgon   mermaid   phoenix   sphinx   unicorn

n o g r o g t x d d
y s d c q j o a k r
g y p d d c r j n a
d b m o r h j r k g
y i s c l q o d k o
p p a d n c i a p n
x g n m i c y h v q
n n g n r n o c d w
i o u f h e u i n b
h m x j n o m h o c
p e y i m f a i r y
s s x r u a t n e c

Follow the tangled paths to find out which butterfly each unicorn is chasing. Write each unicorn's name on the correct line.

The Unicorn Family is out and about doing some shopping.
Look at all that's going on in this scene.

They're still browsing, but if you look closely twelve things have changed. Find and circle them as quickly as you can.

These unicorns need your help to find the right combination to unlock their magic treasure chest. Work out the math problems to find the secret numbers and write them on the blanks.

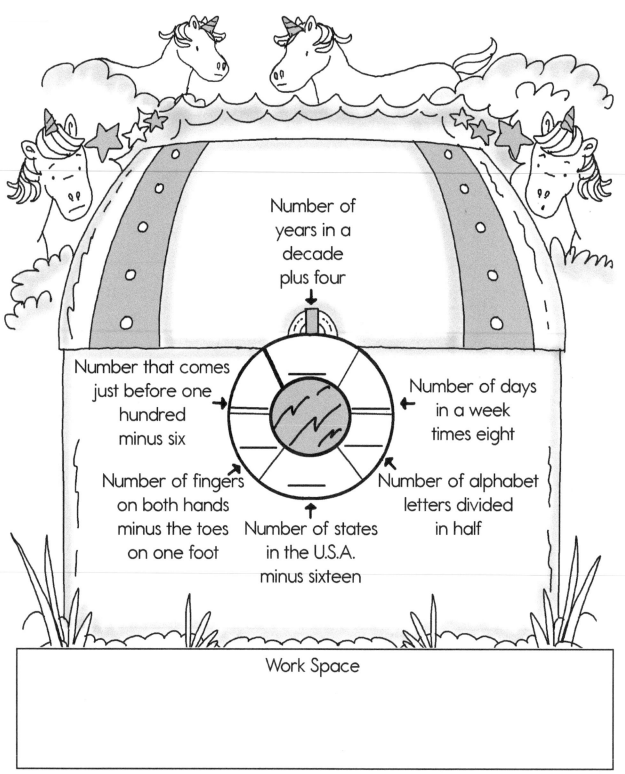

Number of years in a decade plus four

Number that comes just before one hundred minus six

Number of days in a week times eight

Number of fingers on both hands minus the toes on one foot

Number of alphabet letters divided in half

Number of states in the U.S.A. minus sixteen

Work Space

Use these clues to find and circle the unicorn
that will fly over the moon tonight.

1. She has wings.
2. She has a star on her body.
3. She has a short horn.
4. She has straight front legs.
5. She has five letters in her name.

The word *unicorn* refers to a mythological horse that has one horn. And the prefix **uni**, which means "one," is part of many everyday words. Use the definitions below to help you finish spelling more words that start with **uni**.

uni__ __ __ __ __   It has one wheel and you ride it.

uni__ __ __ __   The one outfit worn by a particular group.

uni__ __   To join together as one.

uni__ __ __   Being only one of a kind.

uni__ __ __   Done at one and the same time.

Use the picture clues to fill in the crossword puzzle. A few letters were added as spelling hints.

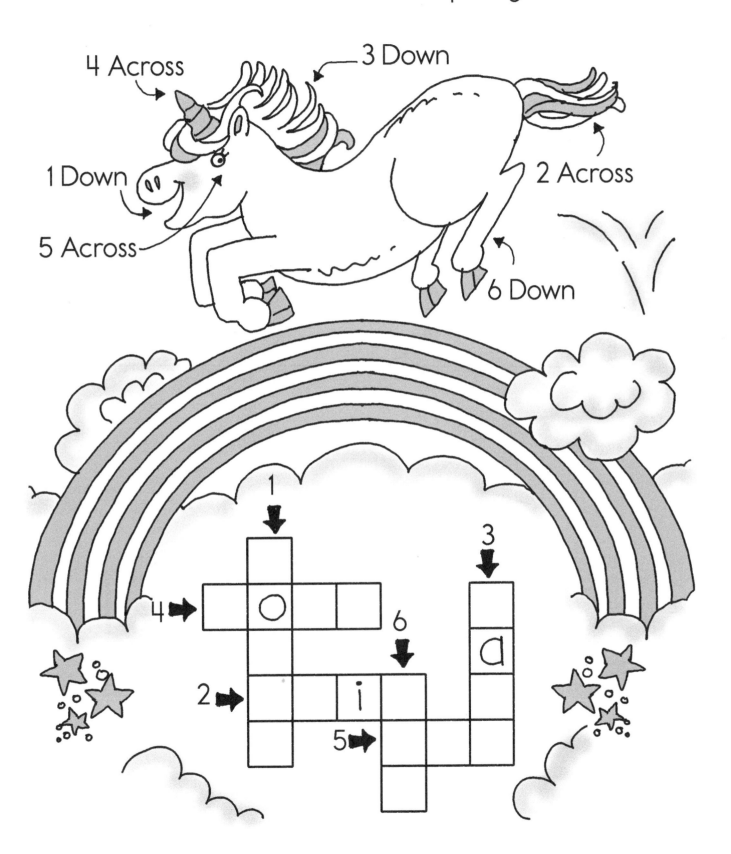

What country chose the unicorn as its national animal? Write the clue letters in the unicorn's horn in their correct places on the blanks to find out.

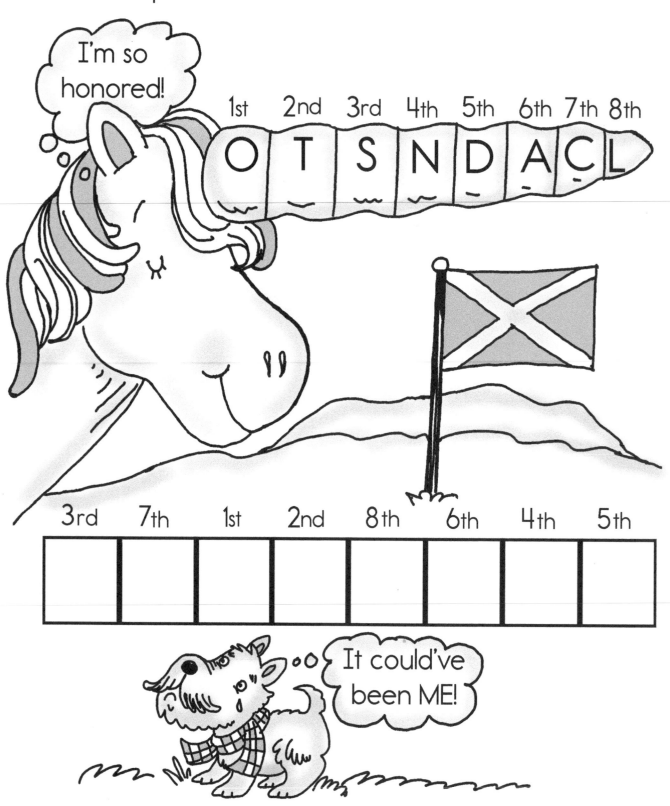

The Unicorn Family is enjoying dessert! Study the picture for a few minutes and try to remember the details. Then turn the page and answer the questions.

Can you remember without looking back a page?

1. What shape necklace is Mom unicorn wearing?

_____

2. What letter is on the ball?

_____

3. What is Baby unicorn eating?

_____

4. What designs are along the edge of the tablecloth?

_____

5. What is the cat licking?

_____

6. What word is on the label of the bottle on the table?

_____

7. What eating utensil is on the floor?

_____

8. What pattern is on the curtains?

_____

9. What number is on Dad unicorn's tie?

_____

10. What is under Mom unicorn's chair?

_____

Try playing this memory game with a friend. Write a new question here.

_____

_____

SOLUTIONS

Connect the dots to create a beautiful creature.

page 1

Unicorns have been here! How many footprints of each kind do you see? Write the number at the bottom.

| 7 | 17 | 4 | 11 |

page 2

Lead this unicorn to a magical place where she can play with friends.

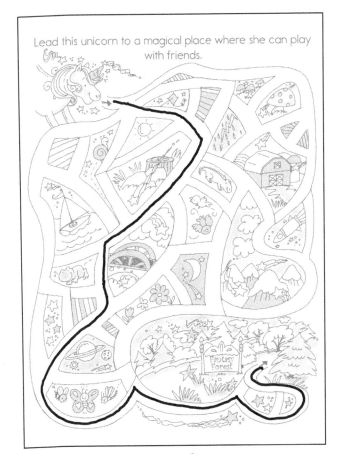

page 3

See how quickly you can find and circle the crescent moon, tent, tennis ball, magnifying glass, spoon, fish, rabbit head, heart, fried egg, and hook.

page 4

Unscramble the letters to spell five words often used to describe unicorns.

sorhe
h o r s e

tfsa
f a s t

ehtwi
w h i t e

nkdi
k i n d

cailamg
m a g i c a l

Make your own unicorn word scramble here!

page 5

The famous explorer Marco Polo once believed that he saw a unicorn! Cross out the first letter and then cross out every other letter after that. Write the remaining letters, in order, on the blanks to find out what he really saw.

I know what you are!

j r b h g
i t n d o
q c p e n
r t o v s

r h i n o c e r o s

page 6

Use the code at the bottom of the page to find the answers to these unicorn riddles.

What's the difference between a unicorn and a carrot?

O N E is a funny **B E A S T**

and the other is a bunny **F E A S T**

What do you call a smart unicorn?

T H E "A" C O R N

Magical Code

☼ = E   🌐 = T   ✎ = N   👁 = B
☆ = A   🪐 = S   🌰 = H   ✦ = R
🪐 = O   ✱ = F   🌐 = C

page 7

Follow the directions to lead the baby to his mother.

Shade in...
3 stars to the right
2 stars up
1 star to the left
4 stars up
3 stars right
1 star down
1 star to the right
2 stars up

page 8

40

Shhh! Find and circle the one sleeping unicorn that is different from the others.

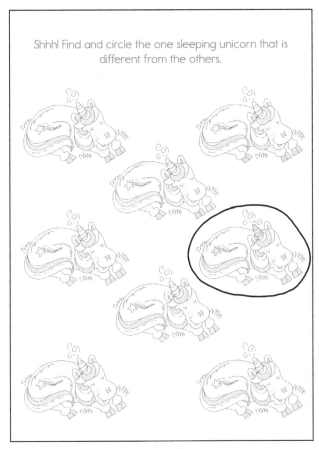

page 9

Look up, down, across, and diagonally to find and circle the word "unicorn" the number of times shown under the rainbow.

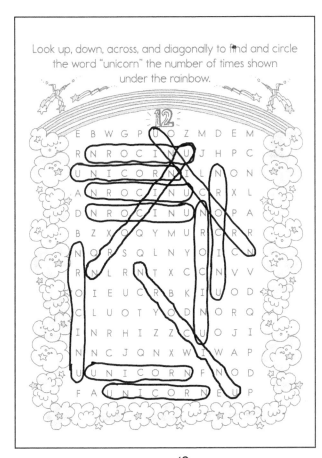

page 10

Write the letter that comes just before the one shown to reveal the name of a sea creature that is sometimes called a "Sea Unicorn."

N ← O
A ← B
R ← S
W ← X
H ← I
A ← B
L ← M

page 11

According to mythology, what special ability do unicorns have? Use the shape code to find out.

△ = A   ◇ = M   ◉ = O   ♡ = S
◯ = H   △ = I   ◇ = R   ▭ = P
☆ = E   ▢ = N   ▭ = G
▢ = C   ♡ = W   ☆ = L

M A G I C A L

H E A L I N G

P O W E R S

page 12

Write the first letter of each picture clue on the space below it. The answer will tell you the kinds of colors that are said to be in a unicorn's mane. Then color the unicorn any way you wish.

R A I N B O W

Legend has it that unicorns can make themselves and other creatures invisible. How fast can you fit the names of these forest animals into the crossword puzzle? Some letters have been included as clues.

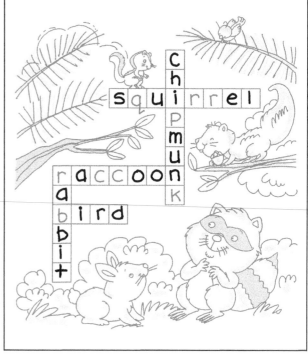

page 13

page 14

Write the opposite of each word on the left. When you are done, print the letters in the circles from top to bottom on the nine blank spaces below. They will spell out what it might be like to ride on the back of a unicorn.

first- las(t)
soft- (h)ard
left- (r)igh(t)
small- b(i)g
shiny- du(l)l
dark- (l)igh(t)
out- (i)n
far- (n)ea(r)
stop- (g)o

thrilling

Use the vowels to finish spelling the message below. It will tell you something interesting about unicorns.

A E I O U

A GROUP OF UNICORNS IS CALLED A BLESSING.

15

page 18

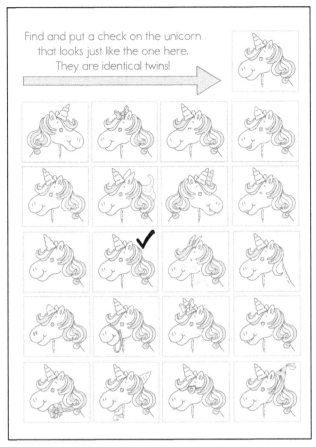

Find and put a check on the unicorn that looks just like the one here. They are identical twins!

page 20

Write the word "unicorn" into the boxes from top to bottom. Those letters will finish spelling seven words that are often used to describe these popular mythical creatures.

fab**u**lous
lege**n**dary
myst**i**cal
magi**c**al
h**o**rse
g**r**aceful
ge**n**tle

You really are awesome!

I really am.

page 23

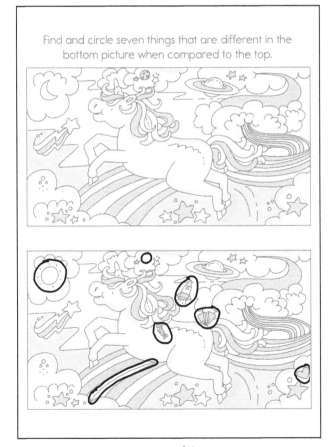

Find and circle seven things that are different in the bottom picture when compared to the top.

page 24

Circle only the capital letters in the flowered frame. Then write them, in order, onto the blanks to find out how long some think a unicorn lives.

unicorns are often shown as white horse-like creatures with a single forehead horn. almost everyone has heard about them.

F O R E V E R

page 25

The unicorn is just one of many popular mythical creatures. Find and circle the names of others you might have read about in well-known stories and legends. Look up, down, diagonally, forward, and backward to find the hidden words.

centaur   cyclops   dragon   fairy   gnome
gorgon   mermaid   phoenix   sphinx   unicorn

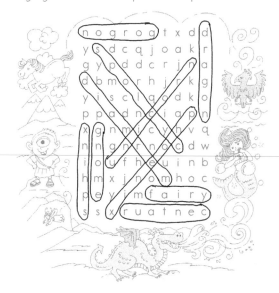

n o g r o g t x d d
y s d c q j o a k r
g y p d d c r j n a
d b m o r h i r k g
y i s c l q d k o
p p a d n c i a p n
x g n m i c y h v q
n n g n r n o c d w
i o u f h e u i n b
h m x i n o m h o c
p e y i m f a i r y
s s x r u a t n e c

page 26

Follow the tangled paths to find out which butterfly each unicorn is chasing. Write each unicorn's name on the correct line.

Sugar   Galaxy   Windy   Spice

page 27

They're still browsing, but if you look closely twelve things have changed. Find and circle them as quickly as you can.

page 29

44

These unicorns need your help to find the right combination to unlock their magic treasure chest. Work out the math problems to find the secret numbers and write them on the blanks.

Number of years in a decade plus four
14

Number that comes just before one hundred minus six
93

Number of days in a week times eight
56

5

13

Number of fingers on both hands minus the toes on one foot
34

Number of states in the U.S.A. minus sixteen

Number of alphabet letters divided in half

Work Space

page 30

Use these clues to find and circle the unicorn that will fly over the moon tonight.

1. She has wings.
2. She has a star on her body.
3. She has a short horn.
4. She has straight front legs.
5. She has five letters in her name.

page 31

The word *unicorn* refers to a mythological horse that has one horn. And the prefix **uni**, which means "one," is part of many everyday words. Use the definitions below to help you finish spelling more words that start with **uni**.

uni **c y c l e**   It has one wheel and you ride it.

uni **f o r m**   The one outfit worn by a particular group.

uni **t e**   To join together as one.

uni **q u e**   Being only one of a kind.

uni **s o n**   Done at one and the same time.

page 32

Use the picture clues to fill in the crossword puzzle. A few letters were added as spelling hints.

4 Across
3 Down
1 Down
2 Across
5 Across
6 Down

```
      1
      m
4 → h o r n    3
      u     6  m
2 →   t a i l  a
      h  5 → e y e
           g    n
```

What country chose the unicorn as its national animal? Write the clue letters in the unicorn's horn in their correct places on the blanks to find out.

I'm so honored!

1st 2nd 3rd 4th 5th 6th 7th 8th
O T S N D A C L

3rd 7th 1st 2nd 8th 6th 4th 5th
S C O T L A N D

It could've been ME!

Can you remember without looking back a page?

1. What shape necklace is Mom unicorn wearing?
   a heart

2. What letter is on the ball?
   C

3. What is Baby unicorn eating?
   an ice cream cone

4. What designs are along the edge of the tablecloth?
   stars

5. What is the cat licking?
   a cupcake

6. What word is on the label of the bottle on the table?
   soda

7. What eating utensil is on the floor?
   a spoon

8. What pattern is on the curtains?
   dots

9. What number is on Dad unicorn's tie?
   3

10. What is under Mom unicorn's chair?
    a mouse

Try playing this memory game with a friend. Write a new question here.